Carry the Knight

by

Miguel Lopez de Leon

ISBN: 0692229035
ISBN 13: 9780692229033

CARRY THE KNIGHT

by

Miguel Lopez de Leon

Table of Contents

Prologue

The young man sat at his desk, trying desperately to avoid the belligerent thoughts that repeatedly echoed in his head. He wasn't good enough, he wasn't brave enough, he had ultimately failed. But above all else, one crystalline thought continuously plagued him . . . he knew that he was completely lost.

The twinkling little fairy, an enchanted, minuscule bodyguard with glistening wings, hovered around the young man as he typed erratically on his paper thin computer, protectively circling her important charge. But her worries were consuming her. She knew that this night was different. He had changed too much. He was too tired. He was too confused. She knew, in her immortal heart, that something was seriously wrong.

The circles under his eyes were startlingly dark, his face was gaunt and sullen, he was drinking much more heavily than usual, and almost every night, he cried himself into unconsciousness. She knew he could not see her. She knew he felt alone. With all her might and will, she wanted to reveal herself to him, to let him know that not only was he not alone, he was honored, respected, and protected by powers that he did not even know existed. Yet it was against every law she knew and memorized, against every protocol she was ever instructed. She also knew that if she didn't reveal herself, if he didn't start to believe in something, in anything, other than the harsh world around him, the same world that continuously kept kicking him down, he would eventually take his own life. His book, THE book, would never be written. It would never be read and loved by millions, and it would never inspire a generation of young people who would one day be the leaders of the future. The absence of his work, his thoughts, and his legacy would change the world forever. Eventually . . . all would be lost. So with profound and unheard-of courage, the tiny glittering Guardian made her choice. She broke every rule and regulation in her realm, flew right up in front of the struggling writer, and revealed herself to him, a beautiful, shining little fairy, with shimmering, fluttering, iridescent wings.

Naturally, the young man shouted hysterically, instantly dropping the glass of vodka he was drinking. And in response to the impossible image that had suddenly visualized before him, he fell violently and clumsily off his chair before fainting in a tangled, pathetic heap on the floor of his messy apartment.

With a deep sigh of knowing resignation, the beautiful fairy fluttered down to him and landed lightly on his shoulder. He was already snoring loudly, drenched in alcohol, and dreaming of a cheeseburger.

She wasn't in any way surprised.

One

Domesticity

(Two Years Earlier . . .)

The young man continued to stir his second cup of hot coffee in front of him as he stared at his computer screen, absentmindedly whispering to himself, "Why is he afraid, why is he afraid, why is he afraid . . . ?"

"Jeremy?" his girlfriend called from the living room in their small one-bedroom apartment. "Did you say something?"

"No, sorry . . . ," Jeremy responded, turning away from the glowing screen to respond to his girlfriend of over ten years. "I'm just not sure yet."

"Not sure of what?" Lily yelled back, this time from the kitchen. Jeremy could already hear the bacon she was preparing, sizzling in the hot pan. Jeremy loved this time of day. He always woke up before sunrise, made himself a cup of strong coffee with cream, and sat in front of his computer to start working on his novel. Hours later, Lily would wake up and start making them breakfast. It was a simple daily routine that they had both grown very fond of recently.

"I'm not sure why one of the characters in my book is afraid, like he's not a wimp, but . . . I don't know . . . ," Jeremy answered, turning back to look at the screen. "Why, why, why . . . ," he continued whispering to himself. Already the scent of bacon wafted into the room.

"You'll figure it out," Lily said supportively, if not a little distractedly, as the sounds of clanking pots and pans became more noticeable.

"Yeah," Jeremy mumbled, lost in thought. "Why, why, why, why, why, why, why . . ."

Jeremy and Lily lived in a quaint, quiet part of the city. They were each other's first serious relationship. As Jeremy forged ahead with a creatively productive, though not lucratively successful, writing career, Lily did part-time work at a nearby bookstore. It was only a few months ago that a publishing company answered one of Jeremy's letters and agreed to read a manuscript for a novel he had written. Although elated at the signing of an exclusive contract for a three-book deal, and the advance payment that soon followed, the reality of the contract soon set in. They loved the initial idea of his story, but he basically had to rewrite the whole thing and make many significant changes to the plot and some of the characters. Jeremy didn't care though. He and Lily were just so happy someone was publishing his book; the details didn't seem to matter.

Looking down to the floor, Jeremy saw their little brown dog, Flouncy, happily sitting next to him. Jeremy was a little surprised, as Flouncy usually made it a habit to drop any activity he had at the time if either he or Lily so much as went near the kitchen, much less caused the whole apartment to smell like bacon.

"Not hungry this morning?" Jeremy asked, picking up the cheerful little dog and hugging him. "Who's da Flouncy? Who's da Flouncy-wouncy? Who's da baby?"

"Breakfast will be ready in about ten minutes," Lily called out, interrupting the unavoidable baby talk session that most canine owners seem to reserve solely and exclusively for their beloved dogs.

"All right," he responded, smushing the furry dog's face gently in his hands.

After meticulously saving all his work on his computer, Jeremy, a slim, tousle-haired, soon-to-be novelist in his late twenties, put Flouncy down gently. He made his way to the kitchen, his happy little dog bounding energetically ahead of him.

Walking gingerly out of their small bedroom and sipping the last remains of his coffee, Jeremy was happy to see that breakfast was already set up in front of the small table next to their kitchen. It was his favorite breakfast food, crispy bacon and scrambled eggs. Albeit simple, little things like this made him happy.

"Sit, sit, sit," Lily said after the two shared a brief kiss. Jeremy loved how much pride Lily took in preparing their breakfasts. In truth, she wasn't the best of cooks. But breakfast was the one meal she did enjoy and excel at making. Jeremy usually took it upon himself to cook them lunch and dinner.

"Yuuuuum!" Jeremy exclaimed enthusiastically, knowing it made Lily feel appreciated. "It looks great! Thank you, thank you!"

"No prob," she happily replied as she sat next to him, a significantly smaller breakfast portion resting on the plate in front of her. Lily was always concerned about her weight despite being petite, though significantly shorter than Jeremy. While Jeremy could be described as slim and attractive, Lily was often described as "adorable," with her slender frame and long blonde hair. They were a quirky couple. They bickered, laughed, and often had long conversations about everything, from the latest celebrity in the news to whether they thought Flouncy needed to go to the vet. It had been long since the days of unbridled passion passed. Instead, they had graduated to a daily expectation of stability, security, and comfort. They were the best of friends and were very content. And as the two sat in their cluttered, charming little apartment, full of old books, framed paintings, and wooden furniture, both still in their baggy, comfortable house clothes, so too did Flouncy begin one of his daily rituals.

"No, Flouncy! Flouncy . . . look at me . . . Flouncy, no!" Lily said, as the little dog impressively stood next to her on his hind legs, begging at the table.

"I was surprised he wasn't here with you while you were cooking," Jeremy said, chowing down on a particularly crunchy strip of bacon. "Isn't he usually all over that?"

"Yeah . . . Flouncy! I said no!" Lily replied, authoritatively pointing her finger at the little dog. "He just misses you when you're writing."

"Awww . . . ," Jeremy said, stuffing scrambled eggs into his mouth. "Do you miss me, Flouncy, huh? Do you miss me?"

With surprising speed, Flouncy scuttled over to Jeremy and was once again begging. "FLOUNCY! NO!" Lily said loudly. Yet there was a hint of laughter in her voice, and the clever little dog heard it. Feigning fear, he sat back on the floor, and with ears pulled back and eyes widened, he began to whimper loudly. "Flouncy," Lily continued, trying not to laugh at this shameless spectacle. "Stop it. I mean it."

And as Jeremy and Lily both held back fits of giggles, the furry little dog rolled onto his back, kicking his little paws up in the air in a demonstration of undiluted canine cuteness. "Hahaha. Okay, fine, just for today," Lily said gingerly, giving the little dog a strip of bacon. Jeremy and Lily were very much aware that they fell for this almost every morning.

Unknown to the couple, and even to Flouncy, a fourth member of their household was flying around the inside perimeter of the apartment, dutifully making her rounds. Her name was Eonie, and she took her job very seriously. Eonie was a little fairy with glistening wings and flowing hair, and she was assigned a simple yet very important task. Protect Jeremy at all costs so that he would write THE book, the book that would end up inadvertently changing so many lives. She did not meddle in his life in any way, unless it directly and immediately endangered his writing of THE book. Eonie was instructed to watch over him in a detached manner, and she knew that it would be a much easier job if she did not personally care about him. Naturally, as the laws of her universe stated, she would never reveal herself to him or any human being. She was his silent, impartial bodyguard, and above all, she was a diligent, hardworking professional.

"WHO'S DA FLOUNCY! WHO'S DA FLOUNCY!" Jeremy repeated in the same loud baby talk, holding the happy little dog up in the air.

"You gonna keep writing?" Lily asked as she cleared the plates and placed them into the kitchen sink a few feet away.

"No, I think I'm done for the day," Jeremy replied, putting Flouncy down. "I woke up extra early this morning, so I got in a good amount of work. I don't want to force it."

"Right," Lily responded as she started to scrub one of the pans already in the sink. "I'm off from work today. You want to go see a movie?"

"Sure!" Jeremy answered enthusiastically. It was times like this that Jeremy was truly thankful for his writing work. Before his book deal, he had an endless array of jobs to help pay the bills. He had worked in a library, a bakery, as a temp, etc. But now, with his advance and Lily's paycheck, he found himself in the enviable position of having many days free just to do as he pleased. After all, the new draft of the novel wasn't due for some months. He had plenty of time to finish it. "How about that fantasy one. What's it called? About the dragon and the fairies?"

"Oh yeah, that looked good!" Lily responded. "We have to go to the groceries though. We need a whole bunch of stuff."

"Okay!" Jeremy said happily. He loved doing everyday errands like that. He enjoyed walking up and down the grocery aisles and getting all his favorite snacks and comforts, while he and Lily continued their never-ending daily conversation. "Yeah, we need more coffee. And I think we ran out of dog treats."

"We're running low," Lily confirmed. "Hey, do you think Flouncy is getting fat?"

"No!"

"No, really! Look at him!"

"Uh . . . well, okay, maybe a little."

"He's fat. I knew it. We have an unhealthy dog."

"He's fine. We'll just walk him more. This dog loves four things—me, you, his walks, and eating."

"That's true," Lily said frankly. "Ya know, they have diet doggie treats at the grocery store. I saw them, you know, for obese dogs."

"Good Lord, he's not obese!"

"That's how it starts . . . I'm just saying . . ."

And so the days passed in this same casually charmed manner. Sometimes they would have lunch out in their favorite cafes. Sometimes they would go to the movies and share a large tub of popcorn and soda, regardless of whether or not they had just eaten. Or sometimes they would just stay at home. Lily, aside from being an independent working woman, also had a surprising domestic side. She loved to sew. She could easily, and gratefully, spend the night sewing herself a new jacket of her own design or simply sew fallen buttons back onto Jeremy's shirts. Sewing seemed to totally relax her, and focus her energy.

Once in a while, Lily's parents and teenage brother would come over and keep the couple company. On these occasions, both Jeremy and Lily took it upon themselves, despite having been together for so long, to still put their best foot forward. Lily would end up meticulously cleaning every inch of their small apartment, while Jeremy would go to the groceries and prepare everything for lunch or dinner, or sometimes even both. Just like Lily liked to sew to relax, Jeremy liked to cook and had grown to be rather good at it. He especially liked to cook for Lily's parents and brother, for although Lily was always careful about maintaining her slim figure, her family had no such concerns. They were big people and big eaters, and Jeremy loved to cook for them. He would make anything from steaks, mashed potatoes, scalloped potatoes, baked potatoes, casseroles, omelets, fried chicken, baked chicken, pork chops, and stews to cakes, cupcakes, puddings, and chocolate mousse. After eating, Jeremy would often bond with Lily's brother, and the two would play whatever video games he had brought along for the day.

Sometimes Jeremy would catch himself pondering over just how grounded he and Lily had become. There was a time when they had several groups of friends and were constantly being invited out everywhere. But as the years passed, they had embraced the quiet comfort of each other's company, and they found themselves drawn into a more modest, reserved schedule. Eventually, they lost touch with many of their friends, as a large number of them moved away, or were in the middle of their own personal relationships. It was perfectly natural, and despite being an only child whose parents lived almost completely across the country, Jeremy was more than content and considered Lily's family as his own.

So with mornings filled with typing away at his rewritten novel, and most afternoons relaxing with Lily or taking long walks with Flouncy, Jeremy truly felt at peace. Sometimes he and Lily would simply stay home at night, make themselves a cocktail, and watch a movie on TV before falling asleep effortlessly. And as the invisible little fairy continued to diligently make her rounds around their small apartment, she would often find herself sitting on the couch next to the relaxed couple, watching the movie with them.

Two

Deadlines

As time passed, Jeremy became all too aware of the looming deadline for his rewritten manuscript. He explained to Lily that he needed to really buckle down and concentrate in order to meet his due date. So as days turned to weeks, Jeremy and Lily found themselves following a new daily schedule. Jeremy still woke up early and made himself coffee; however, he found that their long breakfasts and morning walks with Flouncy not only took too much of his time but also killed whatever writing momentum he had already started to build that day. So instead, Jeremy would just make himself a sandwich and more coffee and continue to work at his desk. He would work throughout the day and well into the night, and although he ended the day exhausted, he knew that it was only a temporary schedule and that when all was said and done, he truly loved and believed in his work.

Every now and then, in the middle of the afternoon, after hours and hours of writing, Jeremy would go to the kitchen, still in his pajamas, and make himself a drink, usually one with vodka. He found that not only did it relax his body after sitting for such long periods of time, it also relaxed his mind. All thoughts of laundry that needed to be done, bills that needed to be paid, and groceries that needed to be bought—all those little nagging thoughts in his head would just sort of blur away, and he would be able to focus even more on his work. It was a gradually acquired comfort, which soon became a habit. One drink in the middle of the day, and that was it. No big deal. Walking to and from the kitchen, he would often find Lily sitting quietly in the living room, dedicatedly sewing herself a blouse, or a skirt, as Flouncy napped serenely beside her.

After a while, Jeremy had decided to stop eating dinner altogether. Sitting at his desk the whole day was not exactly providing him with a lot of exercise, and although he was not a vain person, he still did not want to put on any extra weight. So after a long day of work, he and Lily would just end up snuggling on the couch and watching a movie. Oftentimes, Lily would make them another cocktail, just to relax, and they would both gratefully disappear into the story on the screen in front of them. Sometimes Lily would even have their drinks ready for them before Jeremy had even finished his work for the day, which he thought was a very sweet gesture.

Several weeks later, Jeremy made a triumphant announcement from his desk.

"It's done!" he declared happily. "The rewritten first draft is done!"

"What? What?" Lily asked excitedly as she and Flouncy bounded into the room.

"I finished the book! Now all I have to do is work with the editor to completely edit it, and that's it! They publish it!"

"Ahhhhh!" Lily screamed jubilantly as Jeremy leapt off his chair, hugged her tightly, and lifted her up into the air. "Congratulations! Wow! Finally! That's amazing! I'm going to tell Mom! Yaaaaaay, awe honey, you did it!"

"Yaaaaay!" Jeremy exclaimed as Flouncy barked excitedly from the floor. "I just sent the manuscript to the editor, so I guess the ball is in his court for now. He'll let me know what to do next!"

And for a short while, both Jeremy and Lily were able to spend more time with each other as the editor assigned to Jeremy's book did his part to edit the completed manuscript. It wasn't until Jeremy turned on his computer one morning that he was in for a rude awakening.

"It's here!" Jeremy said as Lily walked over to his desk. "The editor wrote me to tell me not to worry about all the corrections he made, which are in red, but to just take it one sentence at a time and not get overwhelmed. Oh wow, babe, the whole manuscript looks like it's been rewritten in red!"

"But you don't have to agree to all their edits, do you?" Lily asked, rubbing his tense shoulders.

"No . . . I mean, if there are corrections with spelling and grammar, then of course, I'll agree to it. Any other changes to the actual writing are negotiable, but wow, I'm going to have to reread every single word of this."

"I guess that's part of getting a novel published, I mean . . . right?" Lily asked.

"Yeah . . . of course," Jeremy answered, scanning page, after page, after page, covered in red. "I guess it is."

Both Jeremy and Lily were amazed at the time and effort it took for him to proofread and make changes to his newly edited manuscript. Every word had to be considered, every sentence examined. And as the deadline for the polished, fully edited book drew nearer and nearer, Jeremy often found himself skipping all of his meals entirely, sometimes just living solely on coffee and his afternoon cocktails. Editing his work was infinitely more difficult than writing it, and Jeremy tried not to take any of the editor's mountain of suggestions personally. On the days Lily wasn't at work in the bookstore, he would give her a quick peck on the lips on his way to make himself a drink and comment on all her beautiful sewing work. One day, she had made a skirt, a few days later a jacket, then a dress, a blouse, a quilt, new curtains . . . She would also join him for his afternoon cocktail, grateful for the few moments of time that they could spend together before he had to get back to work. Thankfully, Lily's parents and brother would stop by occasionally and keep Lily company throughout the day, and although Jeremy would say hello and spend some time with them, he would quickly return back to his work. In truth, Jeremy was trying not to get overwhelmed by this new process and just desperately wanted to see it through to its end. He needed the book to be finished. Yes, it was hard not spending time with Lily, but after all, it was only temporary.

As the weeks passed by, the initial shock of the editing process became second nature to Jeremy, and soon, despite having lost some weight from skipping meals, he finally finished the fully edited version of his manuscript. And with a palpable sense of satisfaction, accomplishment, and unbelievable relief, Jeremy sent the completed manuscript to his editor. Soon after his publisher received it, the finished novels would be printed for the public. Turning off the computer in front of him, a huge smile plastered onto his gaunt, sullen face, Jeremy looked around the darkened room and realized it was well past three thirty in the morning. Standing up and stretching his weary limbs, he groggily walked into the living room to find Lily and Flouncy fast asleep on the couch. Carefully taking the empty martini glass out of Lily's limp hand and quietly placing it on the coffee table in front of her, he then went to the kitchen and made himself a congratulatory cocktail before gently squeezing himself onto the small couch, hugging Lily, and blissfully falling into a very deep, heavy, and well-deserved slumber.

"To Jeremy," Lily said enthusiastically, holding up her glass to make a toast. "And to his new, brilliant novel! May it be a huge success!"

"Thanks, babe!" Jeremy happily replied. "Couldn't have done it without you!"

"Damn right!" Lily exclaimed with a giggle. "I'm so proud of you!"

As Jeremy, Lily, her parents, and her brother jovially toasted to Jeremy's completed book, another guest at their celebration sat quietly on top of one of the bookshelves in the living room, keenly observing the small party below.

As Eonie scanned the room, the glistening little fairy took note of the varied efforts the couple had done to prepare for this humble yet special occasion. Jeremy had, after weeks of unintentionally growing a beard, finally shaved and had a much-needed haircut, which made a huge difference in his appearance. The cluttered and messy apartment was tidied up, and the nearly empty fridge and pantry were now fully stocked with food and supplies. Lily had put up the new curtains she had sewed, as well as used the new tablecloth and place mats she had made, and had gifted her parents with a beautiful new quilt she had just recently completed. She was even wearing one of the outfits she had designed for herself and was very happy to announce that she had gotten a raise at her job at the bookstore. Everything looked great, Eonie thought; everything was efficient, organized and orderly. As usual, both Lily and Jeremy had put their best foot forward. And although Jeremy had finally completed his book, Eonie knew that it wasn't THE book. She knew that despite the polished appearance of the night's festivities, both Jeremy and Lily had already started to change.

And as the festive night drew to a close, all the delicious appetizers and treats having all been gobbled up, Lily and Jeremy said a fond good-bye to her family. It had truly been a wonderful evening, and the young couple felt extremely content.

"Join me for another drink?" Lily asked as Jeremy started stacking dishes and utensils into the kitchen sink.

"Sure!" Jeremy answered. "By the way, I had a great time tonight. Thank you so much! I loved it!"

"My pleasure," Lily responded warmly as the two shared a long kiss. "My family had a great time."

"Oh, good!" Jeremy exclaimed. "That quilt you gave them was awesome! It's amazing how you can make stuff like that! You should start selling your sewing work. What? No, really! People would buy it in a heartbeat!"

"No, they wouldn't!"

"Yes, they would!"

"It's just a hobby . . ."

"Well . . . you're excellent at it!"

"Aww! Thank you!" Lily demurred as she handed Jeremy back his refreshed cocktail. "To us!" she toasted before each of them took long, drawn-out sips of their strong drinks.

Hours later, Eonie circled the little apartment, fulfilling her usual security check. Fluttering gracefully around, she observed how all the dishes and pots had been scrubbed, washed, and put away; how the garbage had been taken out; and how the whole unit had been tidied up from the night's festivities.

Fluttering down and landing on the back of the couch, a look of deep concern flashed across the shimmering fairy's delicate features. Jeremy was seated on the floor leaning against the couch that Lily was lying on. The young couple were still holding hands and were sound asleep as an empty vodka bottle and two empty glasses rested neatly on the coffee table in front of them.

Three

Dichotomies

Months later, Jeremy found himself at the epicenter of a whirlwind of relentless publicity and marketing. He had spent the weeks preceding the launch of his book starting countless social media accounts, which he had never really done before, and was working tirelessly with his publishing house to spread the word about his upcoming novel. Everything from custom-made business cards to postcards, mugs, websites, prelaunch book reviews, and author interviews were blasted out to the public. Jeremy hadn't even seen a copy of his own book before being interviewed on television for the first time. He had been meticulously trained by the publishing house's marketing team. He had written, and memorized, his own biography, and even knew the questions he would be asked, and the answers that the interviewers were expecting. He practiced over and over again with Lily to make sure his memorized responses seemed fresh and natural. And as Jeremy spoke to hundreds of students at a time at different schools, visited countless libraries and bookstores, and shook hands with and was photographed with anyone and everyone, he eventually grew to enjoy promoting his work. Although sometimes terrifying, it provided a sense of immediate gratification for a piece of literary work that he truly believed in. And although he would return to his hotel room on an absolute high from a great day of work, and would quickly pour himself a drink (by now he already had a favorite, vodka tonics), he still missed his cozy home, his crazy little dog, and most of all, Lily. Although he knew that this initial push for his book was only temporary, he often longed for her company. He called her several times a day when he could, but that only made him miss her more. At first, Lily tried to go with Jeremy to a lot of his book events, but she would inevitably end up alone with her phone in a corner, trying to distract herself while he was being pulled all over the place, either to sign a book or to take a photo. It was, by all accounts, a very good introduction to the public and to the literary community, especially for a first-time author. Jeremy had quickly made a name for himself in a very short amount of time.

But it wasn't until the very end of Jeremy's initial tour, at the end of his final and most extravagant book launch party, that he realized he had to head back home immediately. Jeremy had just gotten back to his hotel room, which was covered with vases of flowers from his publishing house and literary agency. Dozens of his newspaper clippings and interviews were taped onto the mirror above the desk in his room, and he had spent the night signing so many books that he could barely move his right hand. But above all else, what he couldn't wait to do was share the moment with Lily. So after a quick hot shower, he fixed himself his usual vodka tonic, got under the covers of his bed, and called his sweetheart.

"H-hello?" Lily answered, seemingly half asleep.

"Oh, I'm sorry, babe, did I wake you?"

"No . . . no, I'm good. How . . . how was the book . . . um . . ."

"Launch."

"Yeah, yes . . . the book launch. How was it?"

"It was great, Lil! Really, I wish you could have been there. There were so many people and . . ."

"Yeah, I'm really busy too . . ."

"Oh . . . ," Jeremy said. "Oh . . . that's great. Yeah . . . what have you been up to? How's work?"

"How's what?"

"Work. How's work? Babe . . . are you all right?"

"Of course I am! Why?"

"You just sound—are you drinking?"

"Like you're not!"

"Okay . . . yeah, I am. But . . ."

"Jeremy, seriously, the last thing I need is a lecture from someone who isn't even here most of the time. I'm a grown woman. If I want to drink, I'm gonna drink . . . and . . . and I'm gonna . . . I'll do it . . . I'll . . .um . . ."

"Lil . . . ," Jeremy spoke calmly into the phone, "Lily?"

It was only a few minutes later when Jeremy heard her snoring that he finally relaxed. And although he knew the phone bill would cost a small fortune, he held his phone to his ear, until he too succumbed to unconsciousness.

Soon Jeremy found himself back in his little apartment as the whirl-wind of publicity for his novel quickly died down. He was happy with the few hours he devoted each day promoting his book from his computer and was overjoyed to, once again, be at Lily's side. But Jeremy's optimism was tested daily. The woman he left months ago was not the same one he came home to. By now, she was drinking heavily throughout the day. Jeremy tried to get through to her, but she refused to listen, insisting that she was "fine." All the daily rituals that they had, all the everyday errands that he loved to do with her, became labored and exhausting. When they would go to the groceries, Jeremy knew that the first aisle they would hit was the liquor aisle. When they would go to see a movie, he knew she would either laugh, sob, or scream hysterically at the screen. Even when her family would come over, it wasn't the same. She no longer cared if she or their place was a mess and would often be unconscious on the couch by the time her family arrived. Jeremy would make excuses and say she was sick, or had a cold, but it was obvious she was drunk. It came to a point where all of Jeremy's energy was now focused solely on taking care of her, though he had no idea what to do. Sometimes he would find himself so stressed, so filled with anxiety in the middle of the night, that he would pour himself a drink as well, even if he didn't want to. After a while, their cozy, charming apartment felt like a prison. Flouncy's ador-able barking became irritating, and Jeremy couldn't even bring himself to return the numerous phone calls from his parents and literary agent. All he cared about was Lily, and in a way, he became obsessed with her well-being. Jeremy would call her parents and have them stay over, but they were at a loss as well and were incapable of truly helping her. Her mom and dad would spend weeks at a time at their place, but Lily was eventually able to charm them into thinking she was all right, to appease them into thinking she was well enough for them to go back home. And she was . . . for a week or two. Jeremy felt like he was drowning. Lily was deteriorating in front of him, and nothing he did seemed to help.

More months had passed, with even less activity for his novel, and Jeremy found himself in a numbing, chronic, constant state of shock. It was that day, when his patience wore out, that Jeremy was finally broken.

"What? How could this happen? I don't understand. We had a contract . . . ," Jeremy repeated loudly into the phone.

"Jeremy, please understand. It's a difficult time in the publishing industry. Yes, your book did well," Jeremy's publisher said calmly, "but our other books did not. We're closing the publishing house, we have to. If there was any other way to . . ."

"The success of your other books, or your company, is not my responsibility! Where are my checks?" Jeremy demanded, almost in a rage. "Do you know how much work I did to sell those books, how much it cost me and my family? Where are my royalty checks?"

"Jeremy, calm down. We . . . we won't be able to pay you your checks . . . or publish any more of your books. I'm afraid that . . ."

"No, you're gonna be afraid!" Jeremy retorted. "We have a binding contract! You are in complete breach of contract, and the next call I'm going to make is to my lawyer!" he continued, gulping down another sip of vodka.

"Jeremy, there's no need to . . ."

"Are you, or are you not, in breach of contract?!"

"Jeremy, we . . ."

"GO TO HELL, PATRICK!"

After violently hanging up on his flabbergasted publisher and making an erratic, furious call to his lawyer, Jeremy slammed his phone down on the coffee table in front of him, somewhat startled that he was sitting on the floor. Glancing around, he saw Flouncy, cowering in the corner of the room, his little ears shaking.

"Flouncy . . . Flouncy . . . It's okay. Come here, baby . . ."

The dog would not move.

"Flouncy! Come here, now! Flouncy!"

"Leave him alone . . . ," Lily mumbled, passed out on the couch behind him. Jeremy was just relieved to hear her voice. She had been asleep for the past two days.

"What, babe? What did you say?" Jeremy responded as gently as he could.

At that moment, his phone rang. Thinking it was his lawyer, Jeremy answered.

"So . . . can we sue them?" Jeremy said shakily, taking another sip of his drink, as Lily once again passed out behind him.

"Sweetheart . . ."

"What? M-mom?"

"Where have you been? I've been trying to get ahold of you for . . ."

"What's wrong? Your voice sounds . . . what happened?" he asked concernedly.

"Your father . . . he . . ."

"What? Is Dad sick?"

"I don't know how to say this . . . Jeremy . . . he had a heart attack. Baby, he passed away."

"W-what? No. When? I . . . I don't . . . what?"

Although Jeremy and his father were never close, he did love his father very much and couldn't believe what he was hearing.

"Babe . . . Lily . . . ," Jeremy cried out, turning to face her, trying desperately to wake his sweetheart from her intoxicated slumber. "Lil, please wake up. My dad . . ."

And as Jeremy repeated over and over again to his mother that everything would be okay and that he loved her, he continued sipping and refilling his drink, until he slowly passed out on the floor in front of the couch Lily was lying on.

"Dad . . . ," Jeremy mumbled in his sleep, "Lily . . . it's only temporary . . ."

With tears running down her elfin face, Eonie fluttered down onto Jeremy's shoulder and, despite herself, embraced his tear-filled neck.

Four

Diving

Jeremy woke up to his empty, dreary apartment. It had been several weeks since Lily had moved out, taking Flouncy with her. She was a complete train wreck when she had left, and Jeremy was amazed at how she and her family had immediately blamed him for her drinking problem. At this point, her family were his only friends. His mother, now a widow, lived halfway across the country and was obviously suffering depression. She made it startlingly clear that she did not want Jeremy, in any way, to come and visit her. She wanted to be left alone, at least for the time being. She sent him all the information he would need to get in touch with their family attorney as his father had left him a considerable amount of inheritance. And although Jeremy and his father were never close, he still felt this emptiness inside him that he knew would never again be filled. Jeremy would survive, at least, where the rent and bills were concerned, but everything else had fallen apart. How could things change so fast? He blamed himself. It was all his fault.

So for the next few months, Jeremy isolated himself in a sea of repetitive comforts. He tried everything to make himself whole again. The gym, weight lifting, a new wardrobe, redecorating his apartment, getting in touch with his old friends. He gave it a valiant effort, knowing all the while it wasn't working. Even though he had legally gotten back all the rights to his novel, he soon found out that no one else wanted it. His old literary agent had long since stopped representing him, and he had sent his novel to every other literary representative and publishing house he could think of. No one had responded. And try as he might, no matter how many times he sat down in front of his computer, nothing new came to him. He couldn't think of a single thing to write about. He spent a lot of time alone, going about the daily errands that used to be such a joy to him. He would find himself at the groceries accidentally buying Lily's favorite snacks or Flouncy's treats. He would catch himself thinking of his father in the present tense or wanting to call his mom, only to remember halfway through dialing that she would not pick up her phone.

But eventually, Jeremy managed to scrounge together a life for himself. It wasn't easy, but he did it. The man who wanted nothing more than to stay at home with his sweetheart and watch movies suddenly found himself in clubs and bars, laughing at jokes that were told to him by friends he hadn't seen or heard from in years. Jeremy now worked out daily and had gotten in shape. He had a new look and was eating healthier, and he went out every single night in an effort not to be home alone. But other than a shiny distraction, it all seemed utterly useless. Until one night, while out with one of his old friends, Jeremy was introduced to one of the most physically beautiful women he had ever met. From the moment he saw her, Jeremy knew he was, at the very least, smitten. As far as he was concerned, she could do no wrong. As the months passed and they had become friends, Jeremy learned all sorts of things about her that would have scared off any other guy, but Jeremy was steadfast in his loyalty. And for the first time in his life, he knew he had truly fallen in love. He loved Lily, there was no question, but he now knew that he was never really in love with her. Not like this. And as even more time passed, and he and his newfound crush would spend every day together, he finally summoned up what little courage he had left and told her how he felt about her. To be generous and to say the least, the feeling was not reciprocated. And so Jeremy continued to try to do the right thing. They remained the best of friends, and Jeremy knew in his heart that their unusual friendship would someday evolve into something more. It wasn't until the day that she revealed to him that she had met someone else that his world came crashing down. He gave a fantastic act and told her that he was truly happy for her, but in that moment, in that instance, his confidence, in every sense of the word, snapped like a twig. She never had any idea that he was still completely in love with her.

So as Jeremy arrived back at his empty apartment, he lay down on his couch, numb to the events that had just transpired. She was in love with someone else. Despite his best efforts, he wasn't good enough for her. Despite the gym, and the diet, and the clothes, and the redone apartment, he wasn't enough. It didn't help that she insisted he meet her newfound love, who ended up being a complete and utter passive-aggressive worm. Actually, that's the thing that really killed him. Why, of all people, him? She seemed genuinely happy though, with this new guy, this stranger who had known her for all of five minutes. She seemed better, more fulfilled, which, despite himself, made him feel completely inadequate. He had gambled, taken a chance, and lost . . . yet again. And all he wanted to do now was just get really, really angry because at least with anger, his spirit wouldn't be broken, and the sense of loss he felt would not be so acute. But for all his wanting, he didn't feel angry. He just felt ugly. Not necessarily physically, but profoundly. He felt profoundly ugly. And alone.

And as Jeremy passed out on the couch in his living room, Eonie fluttered down gracefully onto his shoulder. She placed her tiny hand onto his chest. Suddenly, his breathing calmed down, and his mind was temporarily at peace. As the glistening fairy settled into the quiet of the night, she slowly raised a hand to her tear-filled eyes as she continued to stare at the dark circles around the young writer's once-boyish face.

Five

Details

As months passed, Jeremy tried to stay friends with the woman he was in love with, but after a while, he knew it was a sad impossibility. It just hurt too much to see her with someone else. And although he knew it wasn't fair to her, he gradually distanced himself from her until they no longer spent any time together whatsoever. Jeremy did it as subtly and kindly as he could, and for the most part, it worked. It just seemed like they were growing naturally apart, as what happens in many friendships. Jeremy felt like an idiot. After all, she had been up-front with him about her lack of romantic feelings for him from the very beginning. It was his own fault he didn't listen. But be that as it may, Jeremy's confidence was still pretty close to nonexistent. He now spent his time alone, busying himself with mundane errands and chores, television shows and books. At night, he would often sit in front of his computer in a desperate attempt to think of something new to write. Sometimes he thought he had a good idea, but it would soon fizzle out. It also didn't help matters that he was now drinking regularly at night, and woke up many a morning with a few pages of writing on his computer that made absolutely no sense at all, just the ramblings of a drunk young man.

One night, Jeremy was once again at his desk, typing erratically on his paper-thin computer. He had had several vodka tonics and had just poured himself another one. Tonight was an especially hard night for him though, no particular reason why, it just was. By this time, he was rather drunk, and he was typing incoherent gibberish onto the glowing screen in front of him. So many thoughts were filling his already-hazy, clouded mind. Thoughts of self-doubt and failure. Thoughts of loss and being lost. Thoughts of not ever being good enough. In short, Jeremy was getting overwhelmed. Very drunk, and very overwhelmed. He was also in very real pain. And as tears fell from his gaunt face, he continued to type seemingly random sentences. Then after another gulp of his drink, it dawned on him that he hadn't eaten the entire day. Suddenly, he was starving. A cheeseburger, he thought to himself. There was a place down the road that delivered. He'd order a cheeseburger and fries, maybe a bunch of them. And after gulp after gulp, Jeremy stopped typing and suddenly stood up, walked around, and looked at his cluttered, messy, unkempt apartment. Even though he had redecorated it, it still reminded him of his past. It reminded him of Lily and her breakfasts, and her laugh, it reminded him of Flouncy and his little paws, all the extra copies of his published, unsold novel were stacked in one corner of the living room, and everything seemed to remind him of his father and of the first woman he had ever really fallen in love with. As more tears continued to run down his face, Jeremy numbly returned to his desk and to his typing. How he longed for peace, he thought to himself in a vodka-filled haze. It would be so much easier to just not feel things anymore. No one would really miss him. No one would probably even notice if he disappeared. People take their own lives every day. It happens. At least those people are at peace, he thought, at least they are no longer in pain.

Suddenly, to Jeremy's complete and utter astonishment, a beautiful, shining, brilliant little fairy, with shimmering, fluttering, iridescent wings, seemed to suddenly burst into life right in front of his face. Shouting hysterically, Jeremy instantly dropped the glass of vodka he was drinking and fell violently and clumsily off his chair, before fainting in a tangled, pathetic heap on the floor of his messy, cluttered apartment.

With a deep sigh of knowing resignation, Eonie fluttered down to Jeremy and landed lightly onto his shoulder. He was already snoring loudly, drenched in alcohol, and dreaming of a cheeseburger.

She wasn't in any way surprised.

The next morning, Jeremy knew he had a hangover before he even opened his eyes. He was starving too. And was he asleep on the floor . .

. again? He didn't want to move. He didn't want to face the day. Another empty, useless day. And what weird dreams he had. A fairy was attacking him with a cheeseburger. So strange. Jeremy forced himself to open his eyes to face the harsh sunlight streaming in through the windows as he pushed his aching body off the floor. Suddenly, a glistening little fairy was once again hovering in front of his face.

"AHHHHHHHHHHHH!"

"Jeremy, don't yell. My name is . . ."

"AHHHHHHHHHHHHHHH!"

"Jeremy . . ."

"AHHHHHHHHHHHHHHHHHHH . . ."

"Jeremy . . . SHUT UP!"

"Oh . . . oh, I'm still drunk. I'm hallucinating . . ."

"You're not hallucinating, my . . ."

"You're . . . you're a fairy . . . a talking one! You're a talking fairy! Oh no. I'm crazy, it finally happened! I knew it would! I'm insane! I'm . . . I'm . . ."

"Jeremy, relax! You're not crazy. You're . . ."

"AHHHHHHHHHHHHHHHHHHHH!"

"This is pointless!" Eonie yelled, amid Jeremy's hysterical screaming. Fluttering closer to his face, which naturally made him even more hysterical, the glistening fairy gently placed a tiny hand on the young writer's forehead.

In an instant, Jeremy stopped screaming. It was the most calming sensation he had ever felt. Waves of warmth seemed to emanate from Eonie's tiny hand, and Jeremy felt completely relaxed and safe. He did not feel hungover, or hungry, or sad, or lonely. Instead, he suddenly felt solid and peaceful and knew that the vision in front of him was real. He didn't know how or why she was there, but he knew she was real.

"Jeremy?"

"Yes?" he answered calmly. The fairy, about an inch away from his eyes, didn't even seem to bother him.

"My name is Eonie, I'm a . . . friend."

"Okay . . ."

"I'm going to take my hand off your forehead, and then we're going to have a talk, okay?"

"Okay," Jeremy limply answered. He felt unbelievably agreeable. "Am I dead?"

"No. No, you're not dead," Eonie replied, hovering backward, away from his face.

"I feel really, really calm."

"Good," Eonie said. "I shared a little of my energy with you. You'll feel like this for at least a few hours. Hopefully by that time, this will all make more sense to you."

"So you're a fairy. I'm sorry, what was your name?"

"Eonie, and I'm not a fairy, at least not in the way you think."

"You look like a fairy . . . and you're twinkling."

"Jeremy, I gave you some of my energy to put you in this state so you'll know that what I'm telling you is the truth, so please do try and concentrate."

"Your voice is so loud for someone so little."

"Yes, well. Thank you . . . I suppose."

"Do you, like, live in a flower?"

"What? Why would I . . . No, I don't live in a flower. Jeremy, I know you feel light-headed, but please try to focus. I'm not a fairy, although I know I look like the ones described in your stories and cartoons. I don't quite know how to explain this to you. There are different creatures all around your world everywhere. They just exist in another dimension as humans do. To use a word you are familiar with, I suppose you would call us 'magical,' but really, we are the very essence of this planet. We are the planet's energy manifested in various physical forms. And although humans can't see, or feel us, we can see all of you."

"Why can't we see you?"

"Because we don't want you to. Humans are not ready yet. You all seem to have a hard time even seeing each other for who you really are."

"That's true. Don't we ever bump into you?"

"We're not on the same plane of existence as you, unless the creatures from my dimension choose to be . . . like what I am doing right now. But otherwise, try to think of me and some of my kind as invisible, silent ghosts who are watching over you. Our main rule that all the creatures from my plane abide by is that we never, under any circumstances, reveal ourselves to humans."

"Okay . . . I don't understand. But you're here now talking to me."

"I know. I've purposely revealed myself to you. But as you can imagine, I have a very good reason to. The creatures on my plane are as varied and different as humans. Some are leaders who keep our kind in order, some are healers who care for the sick, some prefer isolation, and some simply take care of their own families and live simple lives. Many of my kind, though, prefer to spend most of their time caring for the earth and nature."

"Are you all fairies? I mean . . . do you all look like what humans would describe as fairies?"

"Oh, not at all," Eonie answered. "The beings in my world are as different and varied as the animals in yours."

"So . . . unicorns exist?"

"What?"

"Unicorns."

"No, at least not to my knowledge. Though I will never understand the human fascination of a horse with a horn on its head, especially since so many of your other animals have horns. I mean, why isn't it ingrained in your popular culture to have a frog with a horn on its head, or a bird?"

"I don't know . . . what?"

"Sorry, I think I'm confusing you. I might have transferred too much of my energy to you."

"It's okay. It's nice," Jeremy said in a pleasant daze.

"Where was I . . . ? Oh yes. So we all have different occupations. For example, I am a Guardian, a rather high-ranking one, in fact."

"Guardians? What are you guarding?"

"Well . . . you. Guardians are beings who look after specific humans who are destined to do great things. But other than making sure those great things get done, we are not supposed to interfere in our charges' lives in any way. As you can imagine, my speaking to you has broken every rule and law I know of."

"Then why did you reveal yourself? Wait . . . I'm destined to do something great?"

"You are. Something very great. And I have been looking after you for a very long time."

"What am I destined to do?"

"You're going to write a book, Jeremy. A very, very important book."

Even through his enchanted, comforted state, Jeremy could still feel his heart drop a little in his chest.

"I hate to tell you this, but no one wants my book. I mean, a lot of people liked it at first, then they sort of lost interest."

"The book I'm talking about, the important one . . . you have not written it yet. Jeremy, I know you probably don't remember much of last night, of most nights actually, considering how much you drink, but last night, for the first time, you seriously considered taking your own life, and I saw a glimpse of your future. You wouldn't do it immediately, but unless the direction you were headed in was drastically altered, you would eventually kill yourself. This means you would never write the book. And that . . . well, that would change everything."

"What book do I write? I mean, what's it about?"

"At this point, I'm not sure. All I know is that the book you write ends up inspiring many young minds, several of those young people grow up to become leaders in their respective fields, and end up making key decisions that eventually impact everyone in this world. Somehow, the book you write helps get them to those powerful positions. Without your book, they never get there, and other lesser people take their place. They make the wrong decisions, and the results are catastrophic."

"Why can't you just follow the future leaders and just guard them, or guide them or something?"

"That's not how it works. For one thing, the Guardians, what we do, is not an exact science. As of now, we don't know who the future leaders will be, just like we're not sure what your book is about. Also, we have no idea how things come to pass, so our main rule is to not interfere in our charges' lives in any way. If we did, we have no idea if that would change their thoughts, ideas, goals, ambition, and values. By directly trying to help, we might just be preventing them from fulfilling their destinies."

"I'm pretty sure you're changing my ideas of things . . ."

"I know. I also know you can't write a book if you're dead."

"But if . . . ," Jeremy started.

Suddenly, Jeremy looked on in absolute awe as an eight-foot-tall woman hovered through the wall and into the room. She had long, flowing hair down to her knees and was wearing thin robes that seemed to be constantly blown by a nonexistent breeze. The whole effect of the startling apparition was that she was somehow floating underwater, as the currents gently pushed and pulled at her long hair and clothing. She oozed authority, and her entire body was giving off such a bright, golden light that Jeremy had a difficult time looking directly at her.

In a heartbeat, Eonie quickly flew up in front of the glowing woman's face. Moments passed, and although no words were exchanged, Jeremy knew that they were somehow communicating. Before long, the golden woman turned to Jeremy, still sitting up on the floor of his messy apartment, and stared at him with an expressionless face. Then without explanation or reason, she simply hovered back through the wall where she had entered from and faded from sight.

"W-who was that?" Jeremy asked, shocked at the apparition who had just casually flown in and out of his apartment.

"That," Eonie responded, fluttering down to Jeremy, "for lack of a better term, is my boss . . . and she is not happy."

"What? Why? Because of me?"

"No . . . because of me."

Six

Dualities

"Why is she mad?" Jeremy asked concernedly.

"She's not mad, she was just . . . concerned," Eonie responded, hovering in front of Jeremy, who was still seated on the floor. "When I explained why I revealed myself to you, she understood. Don't worry, we're not . . . in trouble, as you would say."

"She's your boss?" Jeremy asked. "She was shining so brightly that I could barely look at her, and she seemed like she was floating underwater! Neither of you spoke. How did you communicate?"

"Her name is Kila. She is the head of the Guardians, and in addition to numerous other abilities, she is also telepathic. Kila is an extremely powerful and respected figure in our world."

"What did she tell you?"

"Well, she was concerned. You have to understand, I have broken every law that my beings adhere to. None of my kind has ever revealed ourselves to a human . . . ever. But when I told her that you would have taken your own life, she understood my decision. She scanned my mind and saw everything I witnessed about you in the past couple of years. And although apprehensive at this unheard-of situation, she knew it had to be done. Jeremy, you're too important to lose. I don't think you quite understand how truly important you are. Anyway, her instructions were simple, brief, and to the point. I am going to help you regain your confidence back, and do whatever is necessary to get you to start writing again. Oh . . . and one more thing. Just as you can see me and Kila . . .

you're now going to be able to see all the other dimensional beings from my world. Just try to remind yourself that they have always been there, and most of them would not even think of harming you. Just try, impossible as it might sound now, to live your life in a normal manner."

"With a fairy flying around me . . ."

"I am not a fairy, I'm a Guardian."

"Sorry."

"It's fine."

"I'm amazed I'm accepting all this information so easily."

"I gave you a lot of my energy."

"Kind of like pixie dust . . ."

"I really don't find that funny."

"Again . . . sorry."

For the next few days, Jeremy and Eonie began a most peculiar and unheard-of friendship. Jeremy, after having several panic attacks after Eonie's calming force on him wore off, soon simply accepted the situation in front of him. He thought it was crazy; nonetheless, he accepted that he was being guarded by a fairy . . . a Guardian. Jeremy was also somewhat concerned to learn that some of the beings in Eonie's plane inherently did not like humans at all. But she appeased him by saying that since humans could not even see them, they just ignored humans altogether. Jeremy was also curious about how long Eonie had been guarding him. She told him that the Guardians only found out about him and his destiny a few years ago. There was a prophecy about a man who would write a very important book, but they had a hard time discovering who it was. Jeremy, apparently, was one of the most important assignments the Guardians had.

In time, Jeremy became somewhat more at ease with this newfound reality, although he still had moments when he thought he had gone completely off the deep end and this was all an elaborate hallucination in his deranged mind. But whenever he had these thoughts, Eonie would assure him that this was reality, and the two would simply continue on with whatever semblance of domestic life they could muster. To Jeremy, he felt like he had gained a great, brand-new roommate, who already knew him inside and out. She knew when he was moody and when to leave him alone, and she knew when he wanted to talk and needed to share his thoughts. In truth, Jeremy was extremely grateful for her company. Eonie too felt a profound sense of relief that she was finally able to speak with the human whom she had been guarding and observing so closely all these years.

And so the day came when Jeremy was finally ready to journey out of his apartment and go to the supermarket. Eonie was in complete agreement. She did warn him, however, that he would see things he wasn't used to and that the best response he could give was none at all.

"When you see beings from my world, just try to ignore them. Just try to go about your daily life like nothing has changed," she reiterated.

"Will do!" Jeremy said enthusiastically. In truth, he was thrilled at the possibilities of what he would see outside the walls of his little apartment.

The short walk to the grocery store was as uneventful as ever. The same bold squirrels were lurking among the trees on the sidewalk; the same quirky neighbors were walking their yappy little dogs. It wasn't until they entered the supermarket itself that Jeremy truly had to pretend he didn't find anything out of the ordinary. Casually hovering on top of the fruit stands of oranges, apples, and pears was a perfectly formed circle of water as big as he was. Walking past it, he could hear loud bursts of sound emanating from the oceanic sphere.

"Ignore it!" Eonie whispered into Jeremy's ear as she sat on his shoulder. "Do not react! And don't look at me either!"

"But what is it?" Jeremy whispered back; he simply couldn't help himself. Of course, it completely escaped both Jeremy and Eonie's minds that Jeremy, as far as all the other humans around him were concerned, was talking to himself.

"He's one of the beings in my world that guard the harvest. They're very friendly. Just get what supplies we came here for and keep walking!"

And just as Eonie and Jeremy were finally at the cashier, Jeremy looked up to see a startling sight. What looked like a human form made completely out of dark shadow was racing toward each person in the room and seemed to be kissing them on the lips.

"What is . . . ," Jeremy started.

"Do not react," Eonie demanded.

And as the shadow figure zoomed up to Jeremy and placed its lips on his, Jeremy felt all the hairs on the back of his neck and arms stand. It was a sensation that was actually quite familiar to him, but now he knew what caused it. So with all his willpower, Jeremy continued to make small talk with the cashier and tried desperately to ignore the kiss of the shadow figure before him.

"What the hell was that?" Jeremy asked as he and Eonie entered his apartment. Jeremy placed the heavy grocery bags he was holding onto the kitchen counter. "I got kissed by a shadow . . . at the supermarket!"

"That," Eonie responded, her glistening wings fluttering in the air, "was a being from my world in charge of finding dangerous humans that the Guardians should keep an eye on. And it wasn't a 'kiss.' It was examining your spirit, your true nature."

"Well . . . I guess I passed the test," Jeremy responded, unpacking the groceries into the fridge.

"I suppose you did," Eonie answered.

"So, what do you want for dinner? I'm thinking . . . some pasta! Spaghetti and meatballs!"

"I already told you, Jeremy, I don't need to eat."

"That's not what you said last night! You almost finished those pieces of ravioli. Okay, then. I'll just make myself a sandwich . . ."

"Wait . . . no, pasta sounds good . . ."

"No, I'll just make a sandwich . . ."

"Jeremy . . . wait! I like pasta . . . JEREMY!"

Seven

Danger

As time passed, Jeremy eventually got used to his everyday errands becoming exciting adventures and looked forward to whatever new beings he would encounter next. He had also gotten quite good at pretending he couldn't see them. From creatures that looked like miniature tornadoes at the movies, to huge, muscular humanoid-shaped beings that looked like they were made of liquid metal at the bookstore, Jeremy was thoroughly fascinated with this strange and intoxicating new world. And even though he was still unsuccessfully wracking his brain at night, trying to come up with new ideas for a book, he felt oddly content. With the constant company of Eonie, and the spectacular distractions that awaited him every time he left his cluttered little apartment, Jeremy was no longer lonely. He also realized, quite to his surprise, that he hadn't had a drink in some time.

One night, after a particularly frustrating couple of hours brainstorming ideas of something, anything, to write about, Eonie and Jeremy decided to take a leisurely walk outside. It was a cool, breezy night, and the fresh air immediately revived the already-drowsy young writer.

"Beautiful night," Jeremy remarked as the smell of honey and flowers drifted past them on the pleasant breeze.

"It is," Eonie responded, daintily seated on Jeremy's shoulder. "I love nights like this . . . the cool air, the bright moon. It's all so relaxing."

"Yeah, especially after sitting in front of the computer for so long . . . I just can't think of anything I really want to write about. Well, except . . ."

"NO! No, no, no . . . ," Eonie quickly interrupted. "I'm not sure what your book is going to be about, but I'm quite certain that writing about my plane of existence and all the beings in it would not sit well with my world."

"No one would believe it was true. It would be fiction. No one would even think twice about it."

"The beings from my world would know. Besides, is that really what you want to write about? Is that topic stirring something in you that it's compelling you to write about it?"

Jeremy knew that Eonie was right. For although the new experiences he was having were fascinating and exciting, in his gut, he knew that it wasn't what he truly wanted to write about.

"No," he replied, "you're right. I'm just wondering what supposedly brilliant thing I'm expected to come up with."

"It doesn't necessarily have to be 'brilliant,'" Eonie replied. "It just has to be whatever you want or feel you need to express. It could actually be a very simple idea, but one that happens to resonate with a lot of people."

"I wonder . . . ," Jeremy started when all of a sudden he saw a figure in the distance that completely captured his attention. Walking down the sidewalk was a beautiful, seemingly naked woman. She had light green hair that reached all the way down to her ankles and had green vines that seemed to be growing all around her slender form. The most shocking feature of the woman though were her glowing red eyes. Jeremy knew that this woman was a being from Eonie's world, and that he shouldn't make it so obvious that he could see her, but for some reason, he couldn't look away. Her movements, even just walking down the sidewalk, were completely hypnotic.

"What? You wonder what?" Eonie asked, looking around them.

Jeremy continued to stare at the vine-covered woman. Seeing him gaze at her, she flirtatiously pushed her long hair behind her ear and stared right back at him, before flashing a dazzling smile. Completely enchanted by her, Jeremy smiled back.

"Jeremy, no! Look away!" Eonie whispered frantically.

In seconds, and with blinding, impossible speed, the vine-covered woman ran up to Jeremy and was almost instantly a few feet away from him. Her dazzling smile and coy demeanor were replaced with a deranged face full of rage and malice. And as the vine woman launched herself at Jeremy, it was obvious that she wanted to tear him apart with her bare hands. Jeremy had no chance to defend himself; she was too fast. He barely had time to realize what was happening before she was nearly on top of him. At the last instance, a sheet of glass seemed to materialize in front of him. Jeremy watched as the vine woman slammed into it and flew backward onto the sidewalk. In an instant, she was once again violently smashing herself against the glass, desperately trying to make her assault on Jeremy connect. But it was no use. The indestructible glass would not waver. Snarling like a vicious, bloodthirsty animal, the vine woman stopped her assault for a few moments and seemed to be studying Jeremy's face. Then in a blur of movement, she was gone.

In a state of shock, Jeremy only now noticed Eonie fluttering next to him, both her arms outstretched in front of her. Looking around him, he now realized that the indestructible glass was actually a perfectly round bubble that completely encapsulated both him and his Guardian.

"Are we in . . . a bubble? Are you doing this?" Jeremy asked, between shallow breaths.

"Yes," Eonie answered quickly, still scanning the area around them for any sign of the savage vine woman. "I'm generating a protective sphere around us. Don't worry, even if she comes back, she won't be able to break through it."

"Who was that? Why did she attack me?"

"Remember when I told you that some beings from my world just inherently don't like humans, but since humans can't see them, they just ignore them. Well, the being that just attacked us is a 'Reet.' Reets hate humans, but like all beings in my plane, we know that since humans don't even know we exist, most of us are impartial. When she smiled at you and you smiled back, she knew you could see her. You have to understand, Jeremy, it's unheard-of, in our entire history, for humans to see anyone from my world. The Reet that attacked us probably thought you were an abomination."

"Why are we walking around at night if there was even a chance something like that would be near us?"

"Think of it this way," Eonie replied, still scanning the area and maintaining the protective sphere around them. "Reets are notoriously reclusive. To bump into one at all, much less in this area, is unheard-of. It would be like being attacked by a gorilla at the movies."

"I couldn't look away from her."

"Yes, a Reet's movements are hypnotic, and as you saw, they can move at incredible speeds."

"She was looking at me, before she sped away . . . like she was studying my face."

"I noticed that . . ."

"This is bad, isn't it?" Jeremy asked, also scanning the darkened sidewalks around them.

"I'm not going to lie," Eonie responded. "Yes, Jeremy . . . this is very, very bad."

Eight

Defenses

Jeremy watched on as Eonie and Kila once again engaged in their silent communication. Kila, still framed by her flowing thin robes and knee-length hair, was hovering above Jeremy as he stood in the middle of his living room, still surrounded by his protective bubble. Even with all the new and varied beings he had seen, Jeremy instinctively knew that Kila was on another level entirely. It wasn't just the underwater quality of her physical form, or the fact that she radiated an almost-blinding golden light. She also radiated power, and above all else, an impartial yet undeniable authority.

Once again, however, after fixing him with an expressionless gaze, Kila slowly hovered through his wall and out of his apartment. Eonie quickly fluttered back down to Jeremy and spoke to him through the bubble.

"Kila was very concerned about what happened tonight, and especially about what has happened in the past few hours since the attack."

"What's happened in the past few hours?" Jeremy asked.

"Apparently," Eonie continued, "the Reets have made sure that word has gotten around that a human can see beings from our world. The news is astonishing some of my kind, but worse than that, it seems to be enraging the other beings in my realm who inherently dislike humans in the first place. To make things worse, word is also spreading that the human who can see us has me, a Guardian, protecting him. News that a human who can see my kind, who is also destined to do something 'great,' is making a lot of the beings in my world very nervous. Some are saying that you'll be the fall of both our worlds. The Reets are making a huge uproar. I'm surprised that they were able to do it so fast."

"This sounds really bad . . . ," Jeremy nervously stated. "So what do we do now? I can't just live in this bubble, can I?"

"No, but Kila was worried that you might become a target. Although I doubt the Reet we encountered knows where you live, she was wandering very close to this apartment. Kila is going to send us extra protection to ensure your safety. Which reminds me . . ."

Muttering under her breath, Eonie's voice grew louder and louder, until Jeremy could hear her clearly chanting in a language he had never heard before. Suddenly, he felt his entire apartment shake and shudder under his feet. But just as quickly as the shaking had started, it disappeared. Jeremy also noticed that the defensive bubble around him was gone.

"The protective sphere is now surrounding your entire apartment unit." Eonie said, fluttering down to his shoulder. "You should be safe here for the time being."

"But what about when we go outside?"

"Kila told me to make sure you stay inside this unit for the next couple of days and to not leave the perimeter of the protective sphere. She wants us to just stay here, at least until she finds a way to calm everyone in my world who knows about you."

"Won't that take a while?"

"She's not sure. This is an unprecedented incident. It's never happened before. Besides, she is eager that you continue on the path to writing your book. Not only will your book fulfill your destiny, but once it is published and read by the masses, it will also make you less of a target. The beings in my world could now be told what your legacy is, which is your book, and not all the world-ending conspiracy theories that the Reets are screeching about."

"Oh! That damn book!" Jeremy said in frustration, flopping himself heavily onto the couch. "Now I'm under house arrest!"

"It's not all that bad," Eonie said, now fluttering in front of him. "Just let Kila handle this. All we have to do is focus on your writing. We can have food delivered here. It will give you the opportunity to really get the ball rolling on this new novel. Try to forget about legacies, and destiny, and greatness. Just ask yourself what you really feel like writing now."

"Okay . . . ," Jeremy replied exasperatedly. "I'll just think of the next few days as a writing boot camp."

"Exactly!" Eonie responded enthusiastically, though with a blank look on her face.

"You know what boot camp is, right?" Jeremy asked.

"Of course!" Eonie replied. "What better footwear to use when you go camping. Boots are very sturdy, I hear."

"What? Wait . . . what?"

"Oh, finally," Eonie exclaimed, "here's our added security."

Out of nowhere, Jeremy watched as a small puppy, no bigger than his beloved Flouncy, happily bounded into the room. With its golden fur and floppy ears, it looked exactly like a baby golden retriever. Happily looking back and forth between Eonie and Jeremy, the jolly little puppy took a running start and tried to jump onto Jeremy's lap on the couch, but didn't quite make the jump and landed heavily back onto the floor. Jeremy picked up the energetic little puppy and put him on his lap. The little dog just stared at him in wonder. This was the cutest dog Jeremy had ever seen.

"Are you serious?" Jeremy started, skeptically looking at the puppy, which was now trying to lick his face. "A puppy? Our added security is a puppy! I'm as good as dead."

"Believe me, Jeremy," Eonie responded, "that's not a puppy."

Nine

Detection

Days later, Jeremy found himself pacing back and forth in front of his computer as Eonie perched comfortably on her usual spot on his shoulder. The little golden puppy, which Jeremy named Plops, happily napped on his desk. Jeremy had decided to move his desk to the living room, thinking that the small change would help get him out of his rut.

The apartment was a mess, and several trash bags were full of empty boxes from the numerous food deliveries Jeremy had sent over. Strangely enough though, it turned out that Plops did not need to eat or go to the bathroom. He was the perfect little puppy; he didn't even shed.

And as the sun set and the light faded, Jeremy went around his apartment in deep frustration, turning on all the lights and lamps that he usually did at this time of day. After all these days isolated in his apartment, he still had no idea what his book would be about.

"Oh! Just . . . forget it!" he declared to himself. And with an unapologetic determination, Jeremy went to his kitchen and poured himself a vodka tonic. It was the first drink he had made since meeting Eonie.

Sitting back down in front of his computer, fresh drink in hand, Jeremy noticed that Eonie had fluttered off his shoulder and onto his desk and that she and Plops were now staring at him strangely.

Taking a sip of his drink, he was startled at how strong and bitter it tasted, yet it was familiar to him. It reminded him of when he used to have a drink when he was writing his first book, and Lily was sewing in the living room. It reminded him of when he was at hotels, and his new novel was being enthusiastically celebrated by everyone he knew. Then of course, that same bitter taste in his mouth reminded him of drinking with Lily, and all those endless nights when he had to drink just to be able to handle her. Then of course, his father . . .

"Jeremy?" Eonie whispered. "Are you okay?"

But Jeremy was lost in his thoughts. All he could see was the girl he was in love with, the one after Lily. Immediately he was filled with embarrassment, and shame. But why? He had fallen in love. What was wrong with that? He told her. He told her how he felt. And even though it was not reciprocated, he had the courage to declare his feelings. Despite everything he had gone through, he still took a chance. "What a mess . . .," he thought to himself. "And yet . . ."

"It's me!" Jeremy suddenly said in astonishment. "The book, the one I'm supposed to write . . . it's my story, with Lily, and Flouncy, and . . . and . . . it's my story!"

"FINALLY!" Eonie declared.

"You knew?"

"Well, only very recently! I had a vision of it."

"Why didn't you tell me then?"

"You had to figure it out for yourself!"

"I just never felt, I don't know . . . like, enough. Like I failed at everything. But I guess . . . I guess a lot of people feel like that. I suppose my story really isn't that unique."

"And . . . ," Eonie continued, egging Jeremy on.

"And . . . I was a mess, but I'm still here. I mean, really thanks to you, but I'm still here . . . And I guess I matter."

"You guess? Of course you matter!"

"And the readers," Jeremy continued, "the book . . . it will convince them that if a wreck like me can survive, they can too. The book will teach them to never give up. I didn't need a brilliant story, I just needed a real one."

"Jeremy, I'm so happy you finally . . ."

Suddenly, the entire apartment was filled with an electric, crackling blue flash, an explosion that hurled Jeremy backward, sending Eonie and

Plops flying in the other direction. Jeremy could still hear Eonie's scream as he smashed into the wall behind him.

"W-what's happening?" Jeremy asked, completely shocked, yet amazed that he could so quickly pick himself back off the floor. In moments, both Eonie and Plops were at his side in the middle of the living room as the familiar protective bubble enveloped the three friends.

"They found us," Eonie said as Plops started growling menacingly at Jeremy's feet. "They're coming for you."

Ten

Demolition

In an instant, all the windows around Jeremy's apartment were surrounded by Reets, but try as they might, the savage vine-covered women didn't seem able to break past Eonie's protective sphere into the apartment. But moments later, Jeremy's unit was filled with other beings and creatures that he had never seen before . . . all apparently intent on killing him. As more electric explosions echoed around the room, Jeremy felt a jolt of energy blast him backward onto Eonie's protective sphere. He felt the sturdy bubble dissolve behind him, before falling heavily onto the floor of his living room. Both Eonie and Plops took a defensive perimeter around Jeremy, and to the young writer's astonishment, the little puppy transformed itself into a giant eagle, then a huge leopard, and finally settled on being an immense lion, defensively protecting its young charge. Eonie was also truly a sight to behold. Although the Reets seemed unable to enter the apartment, a host of various creatures appeared out of nowhere. Jeremy watched as impossible-looking waves of water materialized out of thin air. The dozen waves went straight for him, before Eonie, her skin now a deep shade of red, flew directly into the rampaging currents and pulsed immense amounts of heat from her body that made the waves evaporate into steam. Try as she might to stop all the waves though, too many of them were materializing too quickly around the room, and one of the waves got to Jeremy. In an instant, he was surrounded by water and couldn't breathe. They were trying to drown him. Suddenly, even through the rampaging water, Jeremy heard an immense roar as a huge lion slammed into him and knocked him out of the wave and onto the living room floor. Jeremy gasped for breath as he saw Plops, now stuck in the wave, transform from a lion into what looked like a glowing ball of light, which instantly caused the wave to explode, drenching the entire apartment. Before he could think, Jeremy was once again enclosed in a protective bubble. Jeremy flinched backward as another electric blue explosion hit the bubble but did not penetrate its exterior. Searching for its source, Jeremy saw what looked like very tall walking twig creatures, complete with twig arms and legs, blasting electric currents from their strange stick-thin wooden bodies. Eonie, zooming around at startling speed, flew directly at the twig creatures and blasted them with a tar-like black substance that erupted from her tiny hands. Suddenly, there was a blinding electric explosion as the twig men's wooden limbs were scattered throughout the room.

Hearing something smash into his protective bubble, Jeremy looked up to see several big blobs of green slime, the size of watermelons, attaching themselves to the sphere. They looked like nothing more than gooey masses, until Jeremy started seeing jagged fangs appear from their slimy centers, viciously gnawing at the shell of the protective sphere. Plops, still a hovering ball of strange light, flew directly above the fanged slime masses, before instantly transforming into one of the most bizarre creatures Jeremy had even seen. Catching a glance at his new form before it landed heavily on top of the bubble and the slim creatures, Jeremy saw that Plops was now what looked like a huge silver octopus covered in thick scales that looked like metal. The octopus's bizarre tentacles were ripping the slime blobs off the bubble and throwing them across the room, splattering them against the walls. Jeremy watched as some of the remaining slime beings somehow launched themselves at the armored octopus, viciously biting its thick twisting tentacles with their long fangs.

Completely distracted by the chaos on top of him, Jeremy was startled as someone started pounding on the bubble right in front of him. It was Lily!

"Lily? What are you . . ."

"Jeremy, help!" Lily screamed, still pounding against the bubble.

Suddenly, Jeremy watched in horror as Eonie flew up to Lily's face and blasted her point-blank with what looked like green flame. Lily screamed in pain, holding her hands to her face. When she removed her hands, however, Jeremy saw that another reptilian face, almost snakelike, had taken her place. Shedding Lily's image like a snake would shed its skin, Jeremy saw the creature's true form. It was tall and thin with no limbs, only a snakelike body that somehow stood upright. The serpentine creature suddenly let out a piercing cry that almost instantly knocked Jeremy out. Holding his hands to his ears, the deafening, offensive screeching felt like it was stabbing directly at his brain. The green flame blasts that Eonie was firing at the wailing serpent didn't seem to be harming it anymore. It wasn't until a long armored octopus tentacle suddenly wrapped itself around the serpent and sent it flying across the room that the piercing wailing stopped.

Catching his breath, Jeremy took in the chaotic scene around him. The Reets were still savagely trying to enter the apartment and were smashing themselves at superspeed against all the windows of the enchanted unit. More of the water wave creatures were materializing out of nowhere, and several of the electric blasting twig-men seemed to be putting themselves back together again. The fanged slime blobs, now on the floor, were quickly forming a perimeter around the bubble, and the wailing serpent was slithering back toward the sphere at astonishing speed. Plops, still in armored octopus form, was protectively on top of the bubble, while Eonie was fearlessly zooming around the room, blasting all their adversaries with the same green flames. Although Plops and Eonie were doing an astonishing job at keeping his attackers at bay, Jeremy couldn't help but think how long they could possibly keep up this level of defense. Eventually, they would tire out.

As if on cue, Jeremy's attention turned to the wall across from him. Hovering through it was an eight-foot-tall woman with long flowing hair and robes. It was Kila! And although she looked the same, Jeremy noticed that the golden light she exuded seemed to be pulsing violently around her.

"Jeremy, look away!" Eonie screamed.

Jeremy closed his eyes and turned away from Kila, right before she blasted the entire apartment in a blinding explosion of golden light. Jeremy heard the vine women scream around the perimeter of his apartment, and even though he had turned away and was covering his eyes with his hands, Jeremy could still feel the intensity of the light, the pure energy of it. It wasn't just light, it was a surge of power. And before he knew it, he had hit the floor of his protective bubble; then everything faded to black.

"Jeremy . . . Jeremy?"

Jeremy heard his name being called from a distance, like from the other end of a long tunnel. Was he asleep? For a moment, he couldn't quite recall where he was. He could feel he was lying down, and his hands were covering his face. He didn't want to open his eyes.

"Jeremy?" Eonie repeated loudly.

Recognizing her voice, Jeremy slowly opened his eyes and pulled his hands away. Slowly sitting up, he saw that he was still encased in his protective sphere and that Plops, still a huge armored octopus, was protectively situated on top of it. Eonie was fluttering right outside the bubble at Jeremy's eye level. But what really startled and confused Jeremy was the state of the rest of the beings in the apartment. Kila was hovering at the center of the room, emanating her golden though-now-not-blinding light, as she held the same expressionless look on her face. Glancing around the room, all the creatures that had been savagely attacking them seemed to be transfixed with Kila and were all calmly facing her. Even the Reets, still looking in through the windows of the apartment, were unmoving, quietly staring at the hovering woman.

"What's happening?" Jeremy asked, completely at a loss. "Did she hypnotize them?"

"She's communicating with them telepathically," Eonie explained, still fluttering in front of the bubble, "like how she communicates with me. I can hear them all in my head. They're all negotiating with her."

"What are they saying?" Jeremy asked.

"They are negotiating a deal," Eonie responded, turning toward Kila. "She is explaining to them that you and only you alone are the singular exception to the rules of our world, and that you knowing about us and seeing us will never happen to another human ever again. She is explaining that the destiny you have to fulfill is beneficial for both our worlds, and that if any harm came to you, the planet, and nature as a whole, would ultimately suffer. She is also making it very clear that you are under her personal protection."

"How are they all responding?"

"It's muddled. I'm not sure yet."

Minutes passed as both Eonie and Jeremy continued to stare at Kila, along with the rest of the assemblage. It was so quiet; the only sound Jeremy could hear was his own shallow breathing.

"They've made a deal," Eonie suddenly announced, breaking the silence.

"What kind of deal?"

"Everyone is in agreement that as long as no other humans are granted the power to see us, they'll leave you alone."

"Yeah, right!"

"No, they will," Eonie reassured him. "Kila made them all take an oath that they would keep their word. To take an oath with Kila and not keep it is, to say the least, fatal."

Jeremy watched in surprise as the various beings in and around his apartment slowly started to either fade from view or simply disappear through the walls. Even the Reets sped away from the windows, until only he, Eonie, Kila, and Plops were left in the demolished-looking apartment unit.

As the bubble around Jeremy disappeared, he was startled as Plops, back in his golden retriever puppy form, jumped onto his lap.

"Wow . . . that was intense. My apartment looks like a hurricane hit it. Why isn't every policeman in the city not outside my door? There's no way no one else in the building heard all this!"

"Actually there is," Eonie responded, fluttering onto his shoulder. "The Krus . . . that wailing, serpent-looking creature that made itself look like Lily, it enchanted your apartment so no one would hear the battle. They didn't want any other humans involved or alerted in any way."

"Why couldn't the Reets get past your protective sphere around the apartment, but all those other creatures could? And if they could get past the apartment sphere, why couldn't they get past the bubble I was in?"

"Well, although physically powerful and strong, the Reets are not very . . . I suppose the word that most closely defines it would, again, be 'magical.' They are more centered toward physicality. All the other creatures, all having different abilities, simply materialized inside the apartment's sphere."

"So why couldn't they get past my bubble?"

"As soon as I saw that the apartment was breached, I put a more significant amount of my energy into the protective sphere around you, which is why it took me a little more time to form it. I wanted to make sure no one could materialize inside the sphere with you."

"Is she . . . still communicating with you?" Jeremy asked, staring up at Kila, who was still silently hovering in the middle of the room.

"Yes," Eonie answered, "she is pleased that you have realized what your book will be about, and she is eager that you start writing it . . . immediately."

Eleven

Destiny

Months later, as Jeremy sat at his desk, editing the last few pages of his untitled manuscript on his computer, he was suddenly overcome with a profound sense of contentment . . . and peace. The book was not an autobiography; Jeremy wrote about a fictional character who went through everything he had gone through before Eonie had revealed herself to him. He wrote about a struggling writer, his love and the ultimate loss of his sweetheart, the anger at watching his career crumble, and the pain of his parent's death. He also wrote about falling in love, rejection, beauty, addiction, and despair. And finally, he wrote about rising from the ashes, the value of friendship and self-worth, and above all else, never giving up. The novel was a tribute to courage in all its various forms, and a salute to the everyday man and woman who get up again and again to take on the world. It was a reminder that no one, no matter what they might be going through, is ever really truly alone.

Hours later, THE completed book was finally written, and Jeremy, Eonie, and Plops found themselves just staring at his computer.

"Now what?" Jeremy asked.

"Now you send it out to publishers," Eonie answered. "And you don't have to worry about people not liking it. It will definitely be published. Congratulations, Jeremy, you did it!"

"Thanks, but what about you and Plops?" Jeremy asked concernedly. "I mean, now that I wrote the book . . . does that mean you're leaving?"

"Don't worry, we're not going anywhere . . . ever! Besides, Plops and I like it here. Not only that, but you still need to be guarded. You're still the only human on the planet who can see our kind. I also have a feeling . . ."

"What feeling?"

"That you still have a lot of other books to write . . . important ones."

"Give me a break, I just finished this one!" Jeremy said, laughing.

"Speaking of which . . . you haven't chosen a title for it yet. What are you going to call it?"

"I'm not sure yet," Jeremy responded. "I was thinking of *Carry the Knight.*"

About the Author:

Miguel Lopez de Leon is a novelist who lives in Los Angeles and is the author of the "Galadria" fantasy book trilogy. Book 1, "Galadria: Peter Huddleston & The Rites of Passage" is the first book of the series, followed by Book 2, "Galadria: Peter Huddleston & The Mists of the Three Lakes," and Book 3, "Galadria: Peter Huddleston & The Knights of the Leaf."

Miguel's latest fantasy books are "The Unicorn," "Carry the Knight," and it's sequel, "Dawn of the Knight."

Prior to his novels, Miguel was an accomplished short story writer, even winning first place in Writer's Digest Magazine's "Your Story # 24" writing contest. His short story, "A Working Professional," beat out over 550 other competitors in the international contest.

Miguel's various short stories were published in The Shine Journal, The Oddville Press Magazine, The Cynic Magazine, Fantastic Horror Magazine, The Absent Willow Review, Hungur Magazine, Illumen Digest, Sounds of the Night Magazine, Niteblade Magazine,The Solid Gold Anthology- UK (Published by Gold Dust Magazine), The Cover of Darkness Anthology, as well as seven separate paperback anthologies by Pill Hill Press.

Aside from writing, Miguel's other interests include the real estate business, financial investing, and philanthropic work with several international organizations.

Miguel has also modeled for various international brands, such as Diesel, and was chosen as the main face for a print ad campaign for the Italian brand "Bergamo."

For more info. go to www.miguellopezdeleon.com